NOTE TO PARENTS AND TEACHERS

This book is a purely inspirational, semi-fictional narrative. It describes a personal experience of performing 'Umrah from a young child's perspective. It is not a comprehensive guide. The rhyming text will serve as an aide to the child's memory and the poster and paper dolls provide opportunities for reinforcing learning, but it is expected that parents or teachers will discuss and elaborate further on the text and illustrations according to the child's age and level of understanding.

This book cannot replace a book of fiqh to prepare an older child or adult for the step-by-step obligations of making 'Umrah according to a particular school of thought.

Points that you may wish to highlight in your discussions with children include:

1. 'Umrah differs from Hajj in that 'Umrah can be done anytime and completed in a few hours, whereas Hajj is completed over five days during the month of Dhu'l-Hijjah.

2. The name of the Prophet Ibrahim's son who helped him build the Ka'bah is Isma'il (peace be upon them both) [page 5].

3. 'The One' is a reference to Allah, the One God, All-Merciful and Almighty [page 5].

4. Ihram can be put on anywhere before reaching the point of meeqat: at home, at the airport or on the aeroplane [page 8].

5. The full text of the 'Talbiyah' is provided on the accompanying poster [page 8].

6. Tawaf is customarily completed with a du'a [page 17].

7. During Sa'i, the second part of 'Umrah, there are green lights which mark the area that Sayyidah Hajar ran between while seeking water for her son, Isma'il (peace be upon him). Male pilgrims run between these two green lights, while ladies walk quickly [page 21].

8. According to various schools of thought, it is also permissible for men to cut or trim some of their hair once they have completed their 'Umrah, rather than shaving their heads completely [pages 22-23].

9. Although visiting Madinah is not part of making 'Umrah or Hajj, it is highly recommended and desirable to do so. Most pilgrims traveling from far away try to be sure to visit the Prophet's mosque before or after their 'Umrah.

Also note that an asterisk * has been used in the text to indicate where Muslims should say a blessing after mentioning the name of the Prophet Muhammad* (peace and blessings be upon him) or other Prophet of Islam.

The Publishers

Copyright © The Islamic Foundation, 2010/1431 H
Text copyright 2010 Sana Munshey
ISBN 978-0-86037-458-9

We're Off to Make 'Umrah
Author Sana Munshey
Editor Fatima D'Oyen
Illustrator Eman Salem
Cover/Book design & typeset Nasir Cadir
Coordinator Anwar Cara

Published by
THE ISLAMIC FOUNDATION
Markfield Conference Centre, Ratby Lane, Markfield
Leicestershire, LE67 9SY, United Kingdom
E-mail: publications@islamic-foundation.com
Website: www.islamic-foundation.com

Quran House, P.O. Box 30611, Nairobi, Kenya

P.M.B. 3193, Kano, Nigeria

Distributed by
Kube Publishing Ltd.
Tel: +44(01530) 249230, Fax: +44(01530) 249656
E-mail: info@kubepublishing.com
Website: www.kubepublishing.com

A Cataloguing-in-Publication Data record for this book is available from the British Library

ISBN 978-0-86037-458-9

We're Off To Make 'Umrah

Sana Munshey

Illustrated by Eman Salem

In the name of Allah, the All-Merciful, the Most Kind

Salam, my dear friends,
I hope you're all well.
If you've time to listen
I've something to tell

About the First Mosque,
A beautiful sight,
Which we face when we pray,
Where the *nur* shines bright.

4

It was built by Prophet
Ibrahim and his son*,
And made pure by Muhammad*
To worship the One.

5

My journey begins
With the name of Allah
We're off to make 'Umrah
Labbayk Allahumma!

6

I'm all set to go,
Answering the call
To the House of Allah,
Lord and Master of all.

We put on *ihram*
And wait for our flight;
We'll call the *talbiyah*
When the time is right:

'O Allah, we are here!
Responding to You!
You have no partners;
All praise is for You!'

8

We cross the *meeqat*
And pray *rak'atayn*.
Mom says during 'Umrah
We mustn't complain.

9

The plane has arrived,
Alhamdulillah,
The weather's much hotter
In sunny Jeddah!

10

On the bus ride to Makkah
My eye sheds a tear.
It's hard to believe
That I'm finally here!

11

'We've arrived here at last
For Your sake, O Allah
To visit Your House
Labbayk Allahumma!'

Muslims in thousands
Around me I see;
Skins of all shades,
Like one family.

12

Together, alike,
On the cool marble floor
We pray shoulder to shoulder—
The rich and the poor.

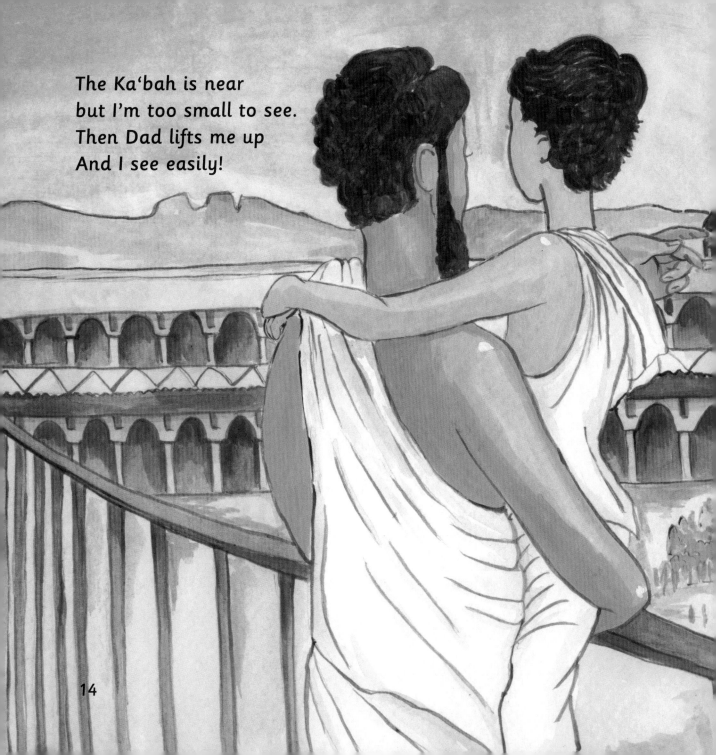

The Ka'bah is near
but I'm too small to see.
Then Dad lifts me up
And I see easily!

14

Now we circle the Ka'bah
We walk and we run;
After seven times round
Our *tawaf* will be done.

15

Each time we go round
Many *du'as* we say.
We greet the Black Stone
As we pass on our way.

We visit the place
Where footprints are seen
Of our Father long passed—
The *Maqam Ibrahim.*

Behind it we stand
To offer a prayer.
We'll never forget
The time we stood there.

We stop for a drink.
Here in Makkah we find
Zamzam water, so good
It's one of a kind!

18

We all drink our fill
Till our thirst is gone;
Then to Safa and Marwa
It's time to move on.

Right up to the top
We climb on Safa;
We raise our hands high
In praise and *du'a*,

'O Allah, You are One;
Your promise is true;
You guided the Prophet*,
All praise be to You!'

20

From there we go down;
Like Hajar, we run,
Who tirelessly sought
A cool drink for her son.

Between the two hills
Seven times we run on;
Our *sa'i* is finished;
My strength is all gone!

21

The next thing's a haircut;
A barber's close by—
Dad gets his head shaved
And then, so do I!

22

The girls also cut off
A bit of their hair.
Now, instead of *ihram*,
Other clothes we can wear.

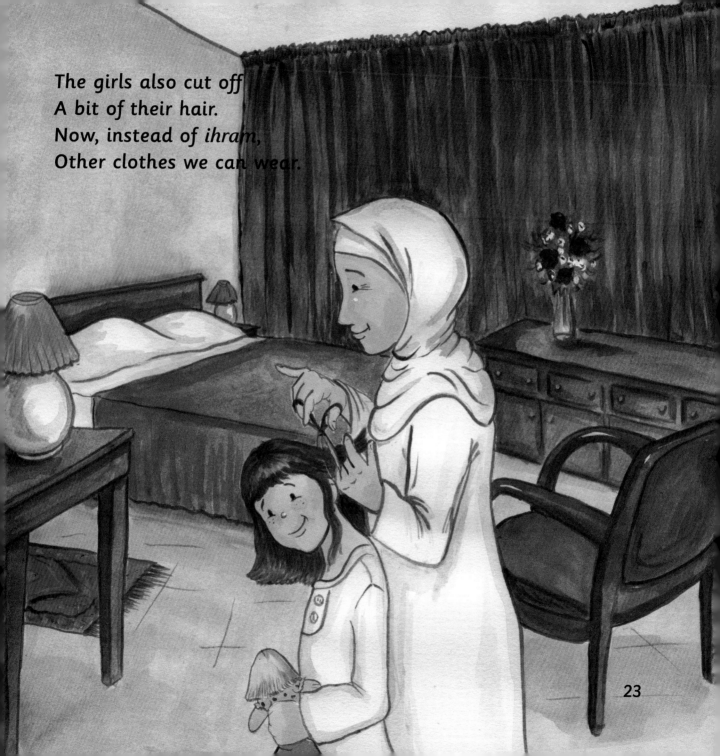

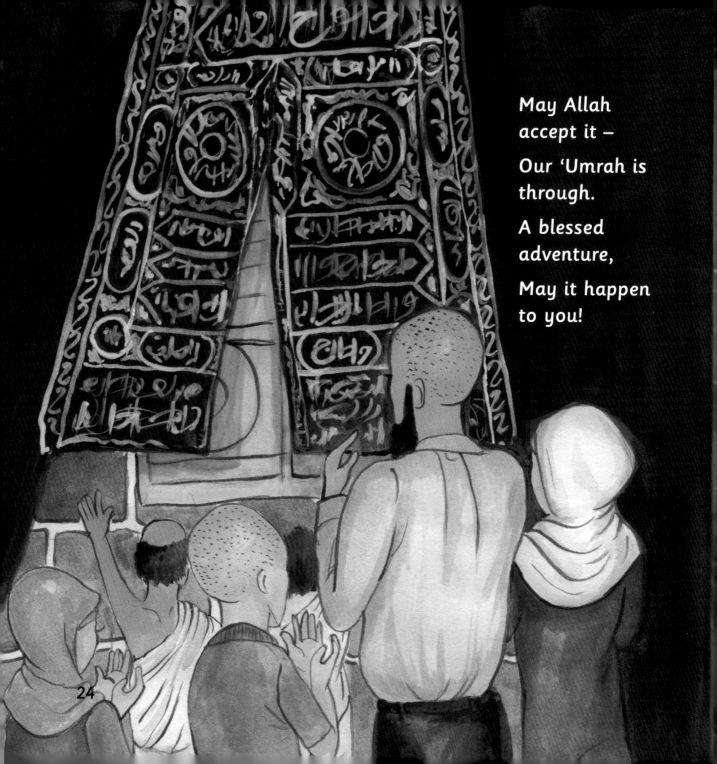

May Allah
accept it –
Our 'Umrah is
through.

A blessed
adventure,
May it happen
to you!

24

Now we visit Madinah,
The city of light;
Say *salam* to our Prophet*
Who taught what is right.

25

We seek Allah's forgiveness

For sins, great and small,

And pray to return

To make Hajj, best of all.

Each day in Makkah,
Again and again
Thousands make 'Umrah—
Women, children and men.

They go, just like me,
To the House of Allah,
Excitedly calling
'Labbayk Allahumma!'

27

Glossary

Black Stone – cornerstone of the Ka'bah; visited during pilgrimage.

Du'a – A personal prayer or supplication.

Hajj – The Pilgrimage to Makkah; the fifth pillar of Islam.

House of Allah – Another term for the Ka'bah.

Ihram – State of consecration and simple outfit of the pilgrim; two pieces of white, unsewn cloth (for males) or loose garments (for females), usually white.

Ka'bah – First house of worship, built by the Prophets Abraham & Ishmael*.

Labbayk Allahumma – 'At your service, O God!'; supplication repeated often during Hajj and 'Umrah.

Meeqat – Locations at which pilgrims must change their clothes and enter the state of consecration, known as 'ihram, before arriving at Makkah.

Marwa – One of two hills near the Ka'bah, visited during pilgrimage.

Maqam Ibrahim – The spot at which the Prophet Abraham* used to pray.

Nur – Arabic for 'light'.

Rak'atayn – Two units of the Islamic ritual prayer (*salat*).

Safa – One of two hills near the Ka'bah, visited during pilgrimage.

Salam – Arabic for 'peace'; also, the greeting of peace.

Talbiyah – The supplication repeated often by pilgrims during Hajj and 'Umrah.

Tawaf – To circle around the Ka'bah, counterclockwise, during pilgrimage.

'Umrah – The lesser pilgrimage, performed at any time of year.

Zamzam – Ancient, blessed well in Makkah.